The Three Bears

Words by Anne McGill-Franzen,
Reading Consultant

Pictures by Sara Cole

RAINTREE CHILDRENS BOOKS
Milwaukee · Toronto · Melbourne · London

About The Three Bears

This book retells a traditional story in pictures. For those who may not be familiar with the story, a brief outline follows page 28. The child need not read the story alone. Rather, adult and child together may enjoy telling the story from the pictures.

Some pages in the book have activities that adult and child can share. These activities are based on some of the themes suggested by the story. The activities will help the child to see books as a source of information and fun. In addition to this element of pleasure, each activity has been carefully designed to prepare the child for situations he or she is likely to meet in the early stages of reading and writing.

Library of Congress Number: 79-62977

1 2 3 4 5 6 7 8 9 0 83 82 81 80 79

Printed in the United States of America.

5

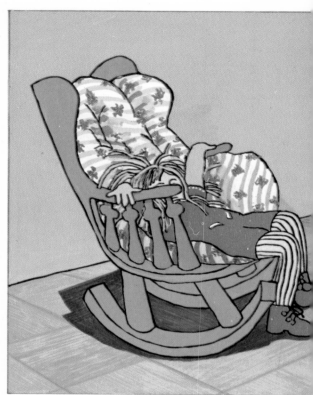

9

b

Can you say 'bears'?

14

What can you see in the picture that starts like 'bears'?

Where do the bears sleep? What do they eat?
What is these bears' favorite food?

How do baby bears play?
How do they keep dry when it rains?

Are polar bears like brown bears? Can you find the differences?

Can you find some big and little things
like this in your house?

Put all the big things on a big chair
and all the little things on a little chair.

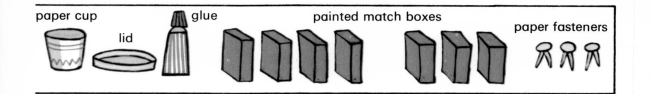

Here is some furniture to make for your bears.

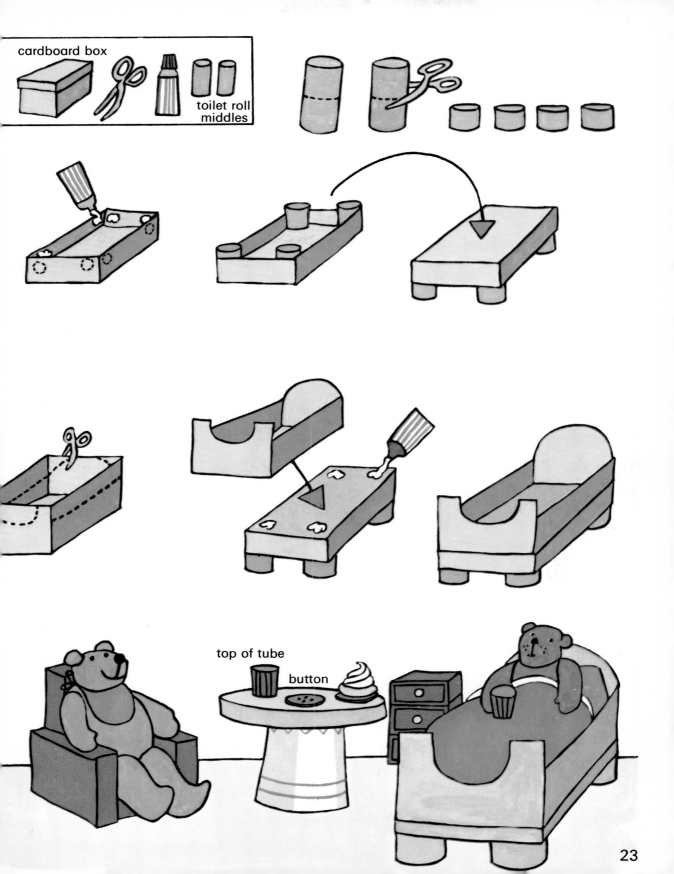

cardboard box

toilet roll middles

top of tube

button

bear

chair

bed

bed

bear

Which things belong to each bear? Which words are the same?

chair

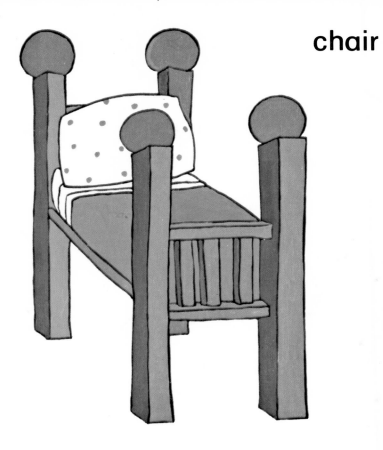

chair

bed

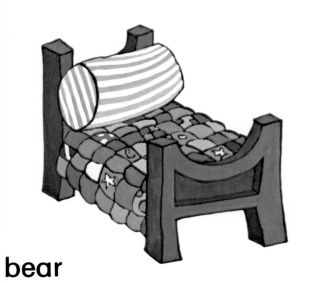

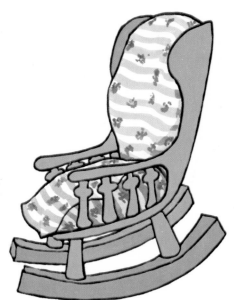

bear

Can you find all the bears, bowls, beds and chairs?

Start at each bear and find his bed.
Go back to the bear and find his chair.
Go back and find his bowl.

28

Story outline of The Three Bears

Three bears live together in a house in the forest—the great big bear, the middle-sized bear and the tiny little bear. They make porridge for breakfast and then while it cools they go out for a walk.

Goldilocks comes across the bears' little house. She peeps in at the window. Then she opens the door and goes into the house. Goldilocks tastes the bears' porridge. *'This is too hot,'* Goldilocks says as she tastes the porridge in the big bowl. *'This is too cold,'* she says as she tastes the porridge in the middle-sized bowl. *'This is just right,'* she says as she tastes the porridge in the small bowl, and she eats it all up. Then Goldilocks tries the chairs in turn, saying, *'This is too high. This is too low. This is just right.'* But the little chair breaks.

Goldilocks explores the house and finds the bedroom upstairs. She feels tired so lies down on each bed in turn. *'This is too hard,'* says Goldilocks, *'This is too soft . . . but this is just right.'* She falls asleep on the little bed. The bears come back from their walk. *'Who's been eating my porridge?'* asks the great big bear in a loud, gruff voice. *'Who's been eating my porridge?'* asks the middle-sized bear in her softer voice. *'Who's been eating my porridge,'* asks the tiny little bear in his small, shrill voice, *'and has eaten it all up?'* The middle-sized bear says she will give him some more. When the bears see their chairs they each ask, *'Who's been sitting in my chair?'* and the tiny little bear adds, *'and has broken it into bits.'* After the great big bear promises to mend it, the bears go to their bedroom. They ask, *'Who's been lying on my bed?'* The tiny little bear adds, *'And look, she's still here!'* Goldilocks, hearing the shrill voice, wakes up, jumps out of bed, climbs through the window and runs away. Will the three bears ever see her again?